For Matthew and Adam

First published in the United States 1990 by E. P. Dutton,
a division of Penguin Books USA Inc.

Originally published in 1989 by Aurum Books for Children
33 Museum Street, London WC1A 1LD

First American Edition   Printed in Great Britain
ISBN 0-525-44562-5   10 9 8 7 6 5 4 3 2 1

NO
BATH
FOR
BORIS

Diana White

E. P. DUTTON ✳ NEW YORK

"Time for your bath," said Mrs. Polar Bear.

"Not me," said Boris.

The bathtub had two faucets.
One said COLD and the other
said COLDER.

"Your bath is ready now,"
said Mrs. Bear. She threw
in a pawful of ice cubes.

"Mothers are always telling you to get into the
tub," grumbled Boris. "And this bathroom's
too hot," he muttered.

Mrs. Bear opened the window so the snow
could blow in.

"Would you like your penguin in the bathtub with you?"
asked Mrs. Bear. The penguin's name was Peppermint.

"My friends like me with dirty fur,"
said Boris, and he crawled under
the tub.

"When you're all clean, you can have a fish lollipop," said Mrs. Bear.

But Boris meant to stay right there for
hours and hours.

"And a plate of fish sticks as high
as an iceberg," said Mrs. Bear.

"Well…" said Boris.

"And a slice of igloo cake," said Mrs. Bear.

"Can I chase the fishermen afterwards?"
asked Boris.

"Last time their husky chased you, you hid under my fur all night," said Mrs. Bear.

Peppermint laughed and laughed,
and Boris looked grumpy.

Boris and Peppermint played their special snowball
game in the tub. Each tried to hit the other on the
nose. Boris kept score.

"Time to dry off," said Mrs. Bear. She took two
towels from the fridge. "Hurry up, or the water
will get warm."

"Mothers are always telling you to get out
of the tub," grumbled Boris.

Boris ate a plate of fish sticks stacked high as an iceberg, two slices of igloo cake, bearberry jam, a fish lollipop, and a cup of cocoa with three spoonfuls of crushed ice.

Peppermint had seaweed salad
and all the sardines.

"Time for bed now," said Mrs. Polar Bear as she brought Boris his cold-water bottle. "Brush your teeth first, Boris. Remember, polar bears have the best teeth of all the animals," she said as she left him in the bathroom.

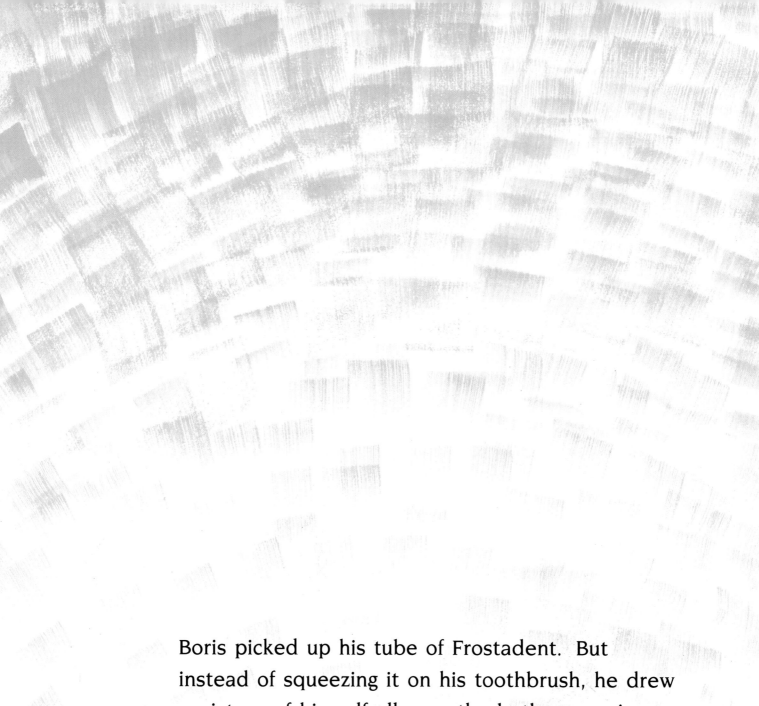

Boris picked up his tube of Frostadent. But
instead of squeezing it on his toothbrush, he drew
a picture of himself all over the bathroom mirror,

and under it he wrote,

"BORIS IS THE BEST."